A Very Hockey Christmas

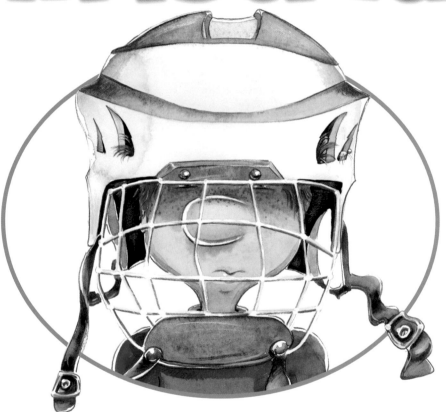

by
Gilles Tibo

illustrations by
Bruno St-Aubin

Scholastic Canada Ltd.
New York   Toronto   London   Auckland   Sydney
Mexico City   New Delhi   Hong Kong   Buenos Aires

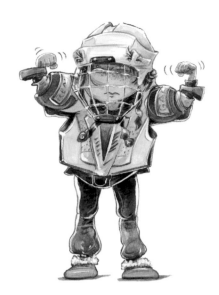

Scholastic Canada Ltd.
604 King Street West, Toronto, Ontario M5V 1E1, Canada

Scholastic Inc.
557 Broadway, New York, NY 10012, USA

Scholastic Australia Pty Limited
PO Box 579, Gosford, NSW 2250, Australia

Scholastic New Zealand Limited
Private Bag 94407, Botany, Manukau 2163, New Zealand

Scholastic Children's Books
Euston House, 24 Eversholt Street, London NW1 1DB, UK

www.scholastic.ca

Library and Archives Canada Cataloguing in Publication
Tibo, Gilles, 1951-
[Noël de Nicolas. English]
A very hockey Christmas / Gilles Tibo ; [illustrator] Bruno St. Aubin ; [translator, Petra Johannson].
Translation of: Le Nöel de Nicolas.
ISBN 978-1-4431-2860-5 (pbk.)
I. St-Aubin, Bruno, illustrator II. Johannson, Petra, translator
III. Title. IV. Title: Noël de Nicolas. English
PS8589.I26N6513 2013   jC843'.54   C2013-902650-9

8 7 6 5 4   Printed in Malaysia 108   18 19 20 21 22

For Marius.

— B. St-A.

It was only four days until Christmas! Nicholas was spinning round and round the Christmas tree, trying to sneak a peek at all the presents underneath.

"Nicholas, you're giving me
a headache!" said his father.
"You're making me dizzy,"
his mother sighed.
"And you're getting on my
last nerve!" his
sister added.

Three days before Christmas, Nicholas tried a more subtle approach. He bent down and pretended to tie his shoelaces, then picked up a present and gave it a shake. He said he was looking for the cat behind the Christmas tree and poked at a few more gifts.

He even did somersaults in the living room, and not-so-accidentally bumped into a box or two.

"Nicholas, if you keep this up, you won't get any presents this year," grumbled his father.

Two days before Christmas, Nicholas couldn't stand it anymore. The wait was driving him crazy! He checked his Christmas list one more time.

Dear Santa,
Please send:
    Hockey jersey
    Hockey gloves
    Hockey socks
    Hockey pads
    Hockey skates
    Hockey books
  Well, anything hockey, really!

Finally, after counting down the days, the hours, the minutes and the seconds, it was Christmas Eve! Nicholas's parents had cooked a holiday feast to feed twenty. But there were only four people in Nicholas's family. What was going on? Were Santa and his elves coming for dinner?

Suddenly, ding-dong! The doorbell rang. But it wasn't Santa Claus.

"Ho, ho, ho! Merry Christmas!" cried Nicholas's grandparents, uncles, aunts and cousins, as they all streamed into the house.

More presents were placed under the tree.
Some of them were even for Nicholas! But
he was not allowed to open them until
Christmas morning.

After a huge dinner, everyone got ready for bed.
The whole family was sleeping over. Nicholas,
his sister and their cousins were staying in the
basement. They played hide-and-seek. They had
pillow fights. Finally, they crawled into their
sleeping bags and fell fast asleep.

11

On Christmas morning, Grandma woke everyone. "Come quick!" she said. "Santa's been here!"

They raced upstairs and piled into the living room. There were presents EVERYWHERE! Nicholas's father started handing them out. His sister got the book she wanted. His cousins whooped with joy as they unwrapped their presents! And Nicholas got the best gift of all . . . a hockey helmet!

But the helmet was much too big. Nicholas's head was swimming inside it.

While his sister and cousins tore the wrapping off more gifts, Nicholas opened another: shoulder pads. Enormous shoulder pads.

Next came a hockey jersey — a hockey jersey for a giant! Then came socks that were far too long.

In the next box were the biggest shin pads Nicholas had ever seen.

Finally, it was time to open Santa's present: hockey skates! But just like everything else, the skates were much too big.

"Don't worry, Nicholas," his mother reassured him. "Feet are what grow the fastest!"

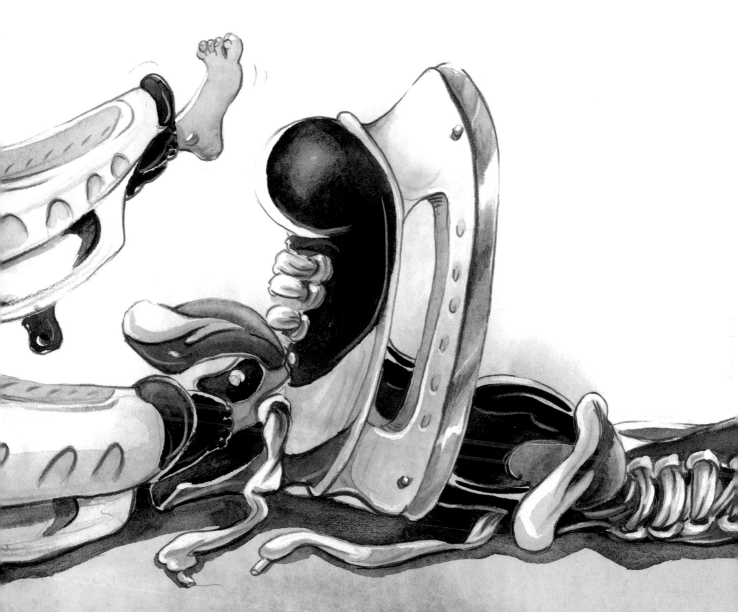

While his cousins ran off to play with their fantastic new stuff, Nicholas sat alone, surrounded by all his too-big, too-large, too-long hockey equipment.

Even though he wasn't feeling very cheerful, Nicholas decided to call his friends and wish them a Merry Christmas. To his surprise, he found out that his friends all had the same problem. Everyone else had received hockey gear, too. Hockey gear that was too big or too small, too wide or too tight.

Nicholas watched the snow falling outside.
Suddenly, he had an idea!

He called back his friends and they all agreed.
It was a fabulous plan!

Nicholas hung up the phone and told his
family that he was going outside to show all
his new hockey equipment to his friends.

"Great idea!" said his grandfather.

Nicholas threw all his gifts
into a bag and ran outside.

24

His friends were already there,
each with a bag of his own.

They dumped out their bags on the sidewalk. All the little players traded their gear with the bigger ones. Soon everyone had new equipment that fit perfectly!

Nicholas went back inside wearing hockey gear that was just right.

The whole family admired him.

"Wow! Nicholas! You look great!"

"Just like a real pro!"

"Everything is perfect!"

"Thank you, thank you, thank you!" said Nicholas. He kissed his parents, his grandparents, his uncles and aunts, and told them it was the best Christmas ever!

Everyone smiled back at him except his
mother, who was staring down at him with
a puzzled look . . .

. . . wondering how Nicholas had grown up so fast!